For Barb Lawton
faithful witness
H.B.

For Frances
J.O.

Grandfather and I
Text copyright © 1994 by Helen E. Buckley
Illustrations copyright © 1994 by Jan Ormerod

Manufactured in China.
For information address HarperCollins Children's Books,
a division of HarperCollins Publishers,
195 Broadway, New York, NY 10007.

Library of Congress Cataloging-in-Publication Data

Buckley, Helen E. Grandfather and I /
by Helen Buckley : illustrated by Jan Ormerod.
p. cm. Summary: A child considers how Grandfather is the perfect
person to spend time with because he is never in a hurry.
ISBN 0-688-12533-6 (trade).
ISBN 0-688-12534-4 (lib. bdg.)—ISBN 0-688-17526-0 (pbk.)
[1. Grandfathers—Fiction.] I. Ormerod, Jan, ill. II. Title.
PZ7.B882Gr 1994 [E]—dc20 93-22936 CIP AC
❖
18 19 20 SCP 20 19 18 17
Visit us on the World Wide Web!
www.harperchildrens.com

GRANDFATHER AND I

HELEN E. BUCKLEY • JAN ORMEROD

LOTHROP, LEE & SHEPARD BOOKS   NEW YORK

*Grandfather and I
are going for a walk.
It will be a slow walk
because
Grandfather and I
never hurry.
We walk along
and walk along
and stop...
and look...
just as long as we like.*

Other people we know
are always in a hurry.
Mothers hurry.
They walk in a hurry
and talk in a hurry.
And they always want **you** to hurry.

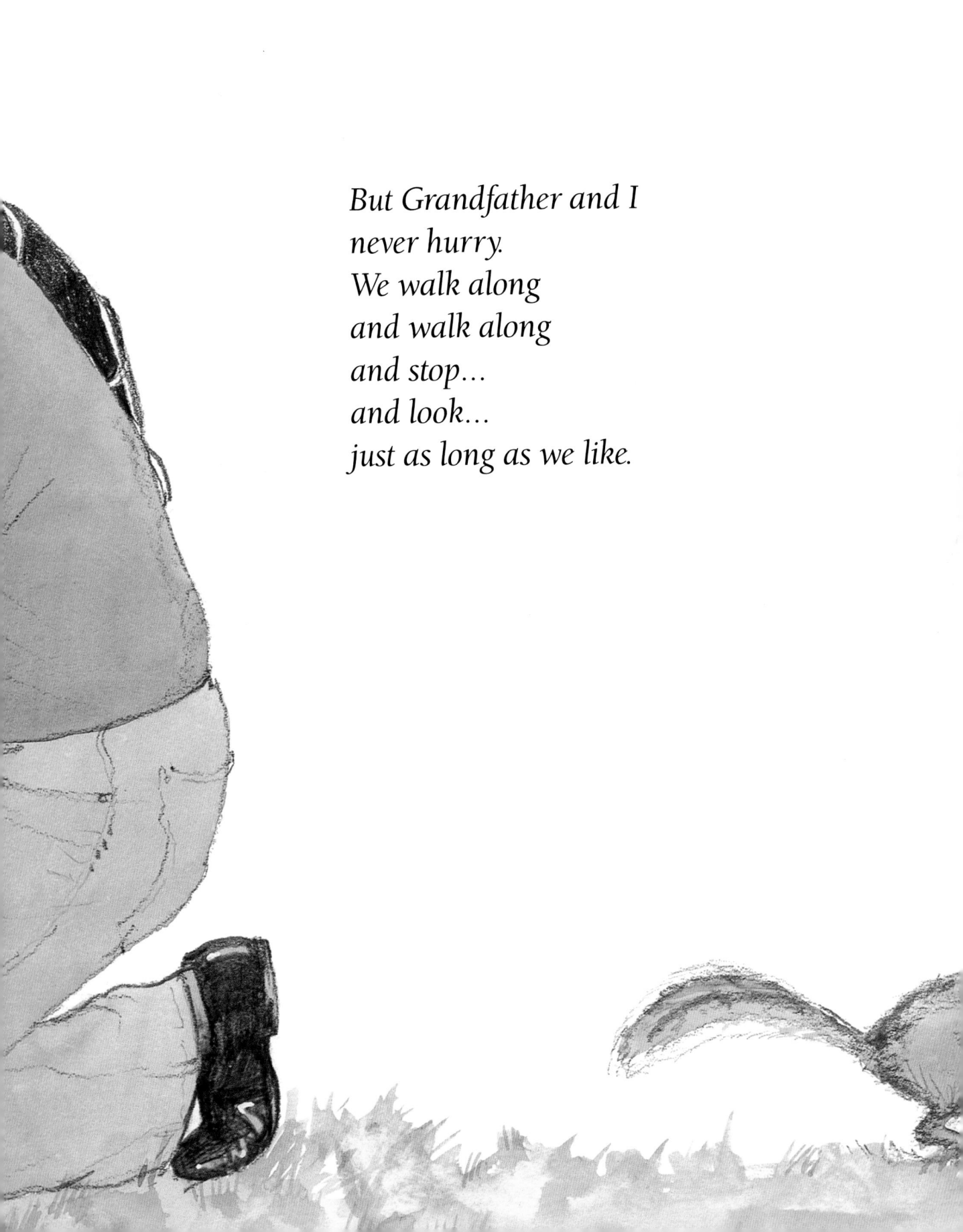

But Grandfather and I
never hurry.
We walk along
and walk along
and stop...
and look...
just as long as we like.

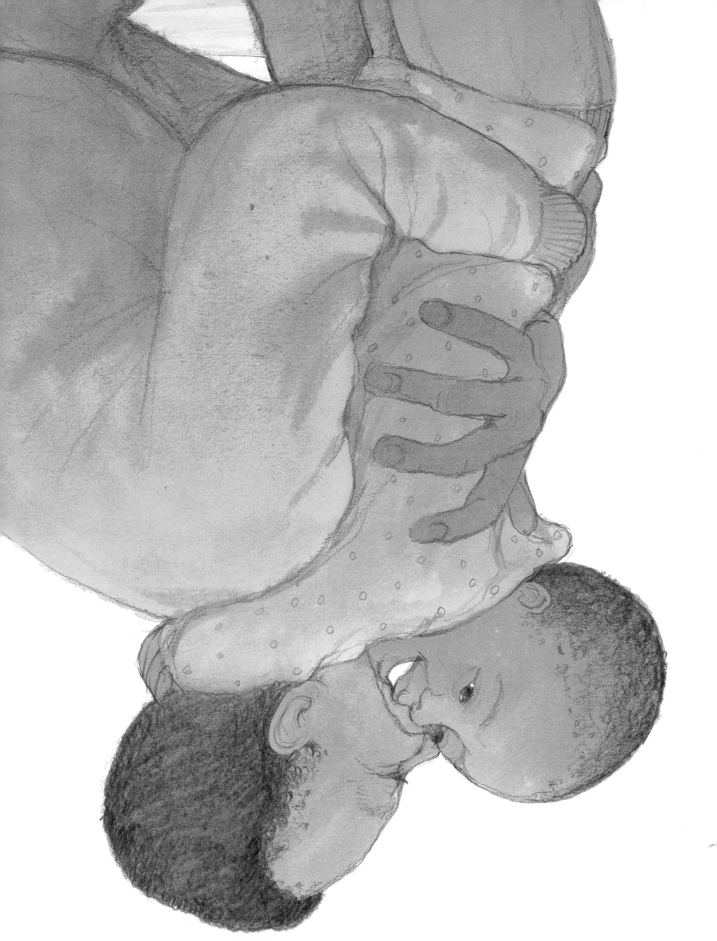

Fathers hurry.
They hurry off to work
and they hurry home again.
They hurry when they kiss you
and when they
take you for a ride.

But Grandfather and I
never hurry.
We walk along
and walk along
and stop…
and look…
just as long as we like.

Brothers and sisters hurry too.
They go so fast
they often bump into you.
And when they take you
for a walk
they are always
leaving you far behind.

But Grandfather and I
never hurry.
We walk along
and walk along
and stop...
and look...
just as long as we like.

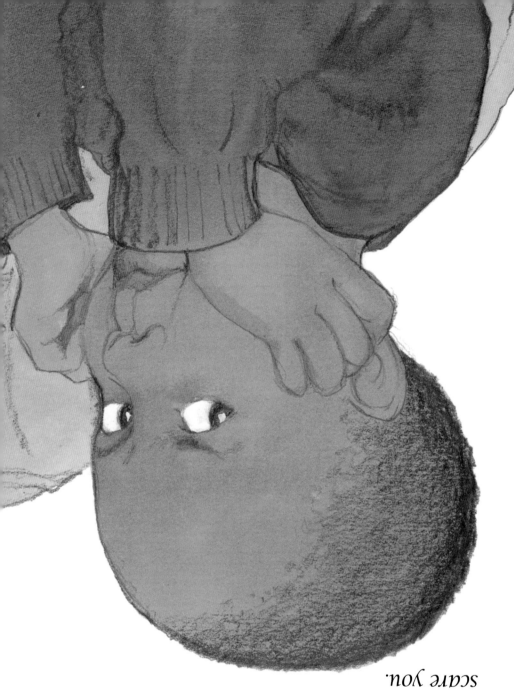

Things hurry.
Cars and buses.
Trains and little boats.
They make noises when they hurry—
They toot whistles and blow horns.
And sometimes
scare you.

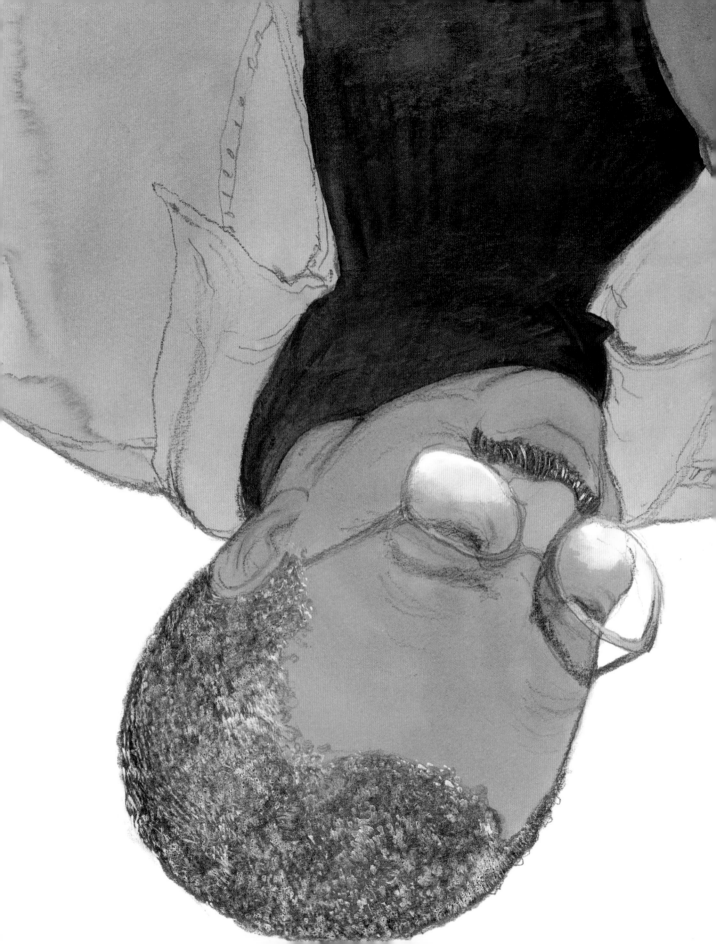

But Grandfather and I
never hurry.
We walk along
and walk along
and stop...
and look...
just as long as we like.

And when Grandfather and I get home,
we sit in a chair
and rock and rock...
and read a little...
and talk a little...
and look...
just as long as we like—

until somebody
tells us to hurry.